CHARLIE

THE SCAREDY CAT

RADA JONES

APOLODOR

This book is a work of fiction. Names, characters, places, and incidents are the product of the author's imagination or are used fictitiously. Any resemblance to actual events, locales, or persons, living or dead, is entirely coincidental.

Copyright © 2026 by Rada Jones

All rights reserved.

No part of this book may be reproduced in any form or by any electronic or mechanical means, including information storage and retrieval systems, without written permission from the author, except for the use of brief quotations in a book review.

APOLODOR PUBLISHING

1

───────

HOME

The only reason hide-and-seek works is that humans don't know how to use their noses. I know I shouldn't peek, but it doesn't matter. I already know where they are.

Unlike humans, I don't look for stuff with my eyes. Whatever I need, I find with my nose, and when I really mean business, I close my eyes to sniff better. Seeing things is just a distraction for us dogs. Everything I know, I learned through my nose.

Still, the kids are fun to watch.

"Ready," Mila shouts.

Tom chuckles.

"Shhh! Be quiet or he'll find you," she whispers.

That's so funny, I wag my tail in a dog smile. Like I don't already know where they are! Tom crawled under the coffee table to hide, but his legs stick out so far I'll stumble upon them if I'm not careful.

Mila squeezed behind the armchair in the corner. She crouched to get cover, but her glittery antlers still stick out. A nose-blind dog could see her with a paw tied behind his back. The kids must have learned how to hide from the ostriches we saw on TV the other day. Those silly birds stick their heads in the sand. If they don't see you, they think you can't see them either. That's just as good as closing your eyes.

But I don't want to ruin their game, so I pretend I'm looking for them as I walk past them to the kitchen where Mom is cooking dinner. We'll have meatloaf tonight, by the smell of beef, eggs, and onions. And that concoction they call Worcestershire sauce, which is just vinegar mixed with molasses, garlic, anchovies, and tamarind. The recipe is supposed to be secret, but a dog's nose knows no secrets. I can even sniff the soy sauce, cloves, and chili oil. Too bad nobody asks me.

"How's it going, Charlie?" Mom is all flushed as she closes the oven. She wipes the sweat off her forehead and spreads some ketchup instead. "Are the kids being good?"

"Yep. Very good," I bark.

She smiles and rubs my ears with her meatloaf-scented hands. I lean into them. I don't mind the smell, not one bit. Especially when I know I'll get my share when she's done.

"Good job looking after them, Charlie," she says.

I wag my tail.

"Don't mention it. That's what big brothers do."

I am Charlie. I'm a six-year-old poodle mix, and I'm Mila and Tom's big brother. Mom says I'm orange, but I don't give a whisker about oranges. If anyone asks, I tell them that I'm the color of cheese slices.

Mom and Dad had no children when they got me, so it was just the three of us at first. But then Mom got really fat, went to the hospital and came back with Mila.

I wasn't thrilled at first. Not only did Mom and Dad get so busy they had no time to play, but the kid screamed all night for no reason. Every night, they wandered about the house like zombies, rocking her to get her back to sleep.

When she grew up, she learned to eat and play, and I got to clean up after her. That was way more fun. Somehow, she became mine too.

Then Mom got fat again. She went to the hospital and brought Tom. He was small, red, and cried all the time, but that was long ago. Now he's bigger than me, and Mila is even bigger, but I'm still their big brother. I look after them, teach them the ropes, and play with them when Mom and Dad are busy.

"I should go back to find them."

Mom nods.

"There's a good boy. The meatloaf is cooking, and Dad should be home soon. Tomorrow's Saturday. You know what that means?"

I wag my tail a mile a minute.

"Sure! No work, no school, so we go play in the park."

"Even better. Tomorrow we are going to cut the Christmas tree. Isn't that exciting?"

I don't know about that. I never understood why they can carry inside a whole tree, branches and all, but I can't even bring in a small stick. And I can't pee on it, either. But I don't want to be the tail that stops wagging, so I do my best to do a dog smile. I wag my tail like I agree, but it swings mostly left, because I don't mean it.

"Sure. Whatever. I'll go find the kids."

They got bored. Mila peeked her head from behind the armchair, and Tom crawled out from under the coffee table.

I leap on him and lick his face. He needs it too, since he's all smeared with peanut butter. He laughs so hard he chokes while I go find Mila. I jump onto the armchair, grab hold of her antlers, and pull them off. She screams, then bursts into laughter.

"You found Tom first. It's his turn."

She has Tom turn his face against the wall and count to ten while we hide.

"One, two, three…"

She squeezes behind the door, and I crawl under the TV cabinet. To be honest, because of Mom's cooking, that space has gotten a bit tight for me, but it still gives me a clear sight line to the door, which I need. I'm in charge of security.

"Eight, nine, ten…"

Tom turns around. He scans the room, then waddles on his chubby legs, looking for us. He opens a drawer — why on earth would he think either of us could fit in there — and gets distracted. He finds his firetruck and forgets he's supposed to be looking for us.

"Vroom, vroom, vroom…" he rumbles, pushing the red truck around the room.

It doesn't take Mila long to get bored.

"What are you doing? You're supposed to be looking for us."

Tom whips his head around to figure out where she's talking from just as the garage door screeches open.

"Dad's home!"

Mila runs out to greet him. Tom follows close on her heels. I'm having some trouble crawling out of my hiding spot. I'll be the last one to hug Dad, but that's alright. That's what big brothers do. Let the kids go first.

2

———

BAD NEWS

I finally squeeze out of my spot and run to greet Dad. He's trying to take off his boots with the kids crawling all over him.

"Dad, Dad, Mom said we're going to get the tree tomorrow! Is that true?" Mila shouts.

Tom pulls on his sleeve to get his attention.

"Wanna see how I play with my fire truck?"

I jump to lick him, adding to the chaos.

"Guess what? We're having meatloaf for dinner," I bark. I don't bother to mention the potatoes. They aren't worth it.

Dad picks up the kids, one in each arm.

"Really?" he says to no one in particular, and smiles, but the smile doesn't reach his eyes.

He looks like he always does when he comes home from work: short curly hair, pressed blue shirt and khakis, but something doesn't smell right. His usual sweet, happy smell turned sour. That only happens when he's upset.

That's how he smelled when Mom had an accident last summer. Also last winter, when Tom coughed so bad he couldn't breathe and Dad had to call an ambulance. He also smelled like this on Easter, when I ate Mila's chocolate egg. The vet washed my stomach, but it wasn't my fault. They left me home alone with it. What else could I do?

But why now? The kids are fine. Mom is in the kitchen, mashing potatoes to go with the meatloaf. I'm fine too.

Still, the sour smell is there without a doubt. Is he sick? I sniff his crotch to figure out, but I get nothing. Well, I get that he's still a boy; he had a healthy poop this morning and a bologna sandwich for lunch. But that doesn't clarify the sourness.

"What's wrong, Dad? Are you okay?" I bark.

But the kids scream at him from all directions, so he doesn't hear me. Then Mom comes from the kitchen. She smells like meatloaf, but she sprayed something all over herself. That's what she does when she wants to smell clean without taking a shower. I don't want to hurt her feelings, so I keep my mouth shut, but she really shouldn't bother. First, because the meatloaf smells fantastic. Nothing smells better than meatloaf, other than bacon. And barbecue. And second, because whatever she doused herself in doesn't cover the food smell, just contrasts it. Now she smells like she's been cooking in the forest, on top of that funky smell she's had lately. Kind of softer, like wool.

She sends the kids to wash their hands. Dad opens a beer, then we all sit at the table, waiting for dinner. Technically, I sit under it, since I'm under Mila's chair. But if she's at the table, so am I.

"What's new at work? Anything exciting today?" Mom asks when the kids fill their mouths with food and go quiet.

Dad works at one of these ginormous stores that sell

everything, from candy and candles to cat food and guns, so something or other always happens there.

Some things are planned, like the taste-testing days. That's when they give away free samples of jam, yogurt, or lemonade. They have "guess the weight" contests, where whoever guesses the correct weight of a melon, a ham, or even a turkey gets to take it home. But unplanned things are more fun. Like when someone tried to camp in a tent in the outdoor department, or when someone else slipped a smart TV under their T-shirt. Once, a bearded dragon escaped from the pet store and hid among the oranges. That caused chaos in the produce section.

"We found a baby in the detergent aisle. On a shelf," Dad says.

Mom gasps.

"In the detergent aisle! Really? Unbelievable!"

She's more shocked that the baby was in the detergent aisle than that someone left him behind.

"Why didn't they leave them with the food? Or at least with the apparel?"

Father smiles.

"You think he'd have been better off with the refrigerated items? Or the fishing equipment?"

Mom's eyebrows join in a frown.

"I'm not kidding! This is horrific! How old was he? And what did you do?"

"It's a she. A few days old, I think. We called the police, who called the EMTs, who took her to the hospital to get checked. We checked the security cameras. Looks like a woman in a hoodie dropped her off."

Mom wrings her hands. Her meatloaf's getting cold.

"That's terrible! How can a mother do something like that?"

Dad shrugs.

"We don't know if she was the mother. And whoever she was, maybe she could no longer afford to look after her. I guess she tried to leave that baby in a safe place where someone was bound to find her before she froze to death. People are struggling out there, Lila. The price of food went up like crazy, but the salaries didn't. Three months ago, when the downtown factory closed, hundreds of people lost their jobs. Many folks have a hard time making ends meet, so they do the best they can."

"I can't believe you'd condone such an act," Mom snaps. Her voice is harsh, like when I come inside with muddy paws. "There's no plausible excuse for doing something like this." She starts clearing the dinner table without touching her meatloaf.

It's hard to believe, but Dad stinks even worse than when he got home. It's a fermented smell, something between pickles, sauerkraut, and stale beer — none of them my favorite. I'm getting ready to investigate him closer when Mom calls me to the kitchen. She needs me to help clean the plates after dinner. That's one of my responsibilities, and I take it seriously, especially after meatloaf.

I get busy with that. Then the kids run to catch me, and I forget about checking on Dad. I only remember when I'm in Mila's room. Mom and Dad's bedroom door is already closed.

I promise myself I'll check on him first thing in the morning and go to sleep.

3
____

FIRED

I told myself that I'd investigate the problem in the morning, but then the day got so exciting I forgot.

Saturday breakfast was a serious affair. We had fried eggs, buttered toast, crispy bacon, and orange juice. I don't give a cat's whisker about orange juice, but bacon? Now you're talking. I wolfed down three slices of crispy, fragrant bacon by myself. I wasn't supposed to, but the kids slipped them to me under the table, so I had to help them out. And they smelled too delicious to resist.

But having all that on top of my food turned out to be a mistake. My stomach flipped as I finished cleaning the crumbs off the floor. I ran to the door and barely made it outside without messing up the carpet.

I pooped and re-pooped, so I was much better by lunch when we went to get the tree. We didn't go to Dad's store where they have those fake things made of green paper and plastic; we drove somewhere where real trees grew right out of the ground. There were so many I couldn't mark them all, but I did my best while Dad and the kids measured the trees with a long stick and debated which one to get.

When I ran out of juice, I tried to grab Dad's measuring stick, but he wouldn't let me have it, so I had to get my own.

The tree they chose was green and taller than Dad, and it smelled of resin and moist earth. I tried to taste it, but it was so prickly that I couldn't tell who bit whom.

We took turns shaking off the snow, then Dad cut it down with his saw, tied it with rope, and strapped it to the car.

We went home. He set it in the living room, then sat on the sofa with a beer and watched the kids hang shiny stuff on the branches. What a cool new game, I thought. I jumped to take them off, but they shooed me away, so I lay down with my nose on my paws to watch them and listen to them sing. The noise was terrible and my tummy was still wonky, but it was good to see them happy. Even Dad, who smelled so bad before, seemed to get over whatever bothered him.

Santa came a few days later and brought lots of gifts: the kids got new toys, coats, and boots. I got a big smoked bone to chew on, but Mom and Dad got very little. They smiled as they watched the kids unwrap their toys, but they both smelled sad, as if the joy had fizzled out of them. Probably because they got so little.

After that, Dad stayed home more than usual. His sour smell never went away, not even when he showered, and I couldn't figure out why. That's why I crept into their bedroom and crawled under their bed this evening.

I listen to them talk. I don't understand many words, but I can smell the badness in the air. Something is terribly wrong.

"We shouldn't have spent so much on Christmas." Mom's voice cracks with worry. "Not now that you're out of a job. We should have gotten just a thing or two for each, and saved the rest."

Dad sighs.

"You're probably right, but I couldn't bring myself to disappoint them. Not now that it might be the last Christmas we spend here."

"The last Christmas here? What do you mean?" Mom asked, her voice shrill.

Dad cleared his throat.

"Lila, I'm afraid we'll have to move. We can't afford to stay here without a job, and there are no jobs to be had around here. Everyone's looking. Our store closed; others are about to shut down. I think we'll have to go north. The economy is better up there. We should be able to find some place that needs someone with my credentials and experience."

"But we can't move! The kids will be devastated to leave their friends. And I just planted the garden. And the hothouse. I even planted herbs — basil, rosemary, mint, and cilantro. We can't leave now."

"I'm sorry, Lila. I tried everything, even McDonald's, but they didn't want me. They said I'm overqualified."

Mom sits up.

"I should try too. I bet they'd take me. At least until you find something."

Dad shakes his head.

"Not now, Lila. You can't. Not with the baby coming soon. There's nothing more important than your health. And the kids."

Mom sobs. "I thought this was our forever home. I hoped we'd talk to the landlord about a rent-to-own deal."

Dad reaches out to hold her. "I know, sweetheart. I'm

sorry. But I'm sure we'll find another place. We'll figure it out, one day at a time."

"But where?"

"I don't know yet. I'll have to find a job first. Then we'll look for a place to live."

Mom sighs.

"It won't be easy, with three kids and a dog."

Dad clears his throat again.

"Lila, I'm afraid Charlie will have to go."

4

————

LEFT

My ears perk up. Charlie has to go? Go where?

My tail wags with excitement.

"Let's go!" are some of the best human words I know. Whenever Dad says, "Charlie, let's go," I rush to the door. Sometimes we only go to the mailbox. Dad waits for me to do my business while I read my friends' peemails. Other times we go for a walk, to the dog park, or even for a hike if the weather is good and the kids have no school. I even love going for rides in the truck to get coffee or gas. I don't care where we go as long as we go together.

I'm about to rush to the door when I remember I'm not supposed to be here. I'm supposed to be in the other room, looking after the kids. I'd better keep quiet. I flatten to the ground to listen.

Mom gasps.

"What are you talking about? We've had Charlie since he was a pup. Where can he go? He has no one else but us."

"I don't know." Dad sounds like that balloon I bit the other day when all the air fizzled out of it. "I asked around to see if anyone wanted him, but I got no takers. I even put an ad in the paper. Nothing. Everyone's struggling to stay afloat these days. I'll keep trying, but if nothing comes of it, I'm afraid we'll have to surrender him to the shelter."

"But why? He's just a little pup! He doesn't eat that much — mostly table scraps, and…"

"Lila, it's not that, even though having a dog is not cheap. Vet bills add up. Even more so as he'll get older. The bigger problem is with the house. Most rental owners don't allow dogs, and those who do will ask for an extra security deposit we can't afford. We don't have that money, Lila. Our chances of finding an affordable, decent place to live are better without the dog."

Mom sobs. Dad tries to comfort her, but he sobs too. I want to go lick their noses, but I'm afraid they'll be mad I snuck in, so I stay put, wondering what's going on.

But days passed, and nothing happened. Everything will turn out okay, I decided, even though the house still smelled sour. The kids and I had a great time that winter, but Dad smelled worried and Mom got fat again.

Then they started packing. The boxes took over the house, and that was fun. The kids and I played hide-and-seek and chased each other around them until they all got filled with toys, clothes, and dishes. The kids watched wide-eyed as their lives got packed into boxes.

"Where are we going?" Mila asked.

"To a place with lots of snow. Do you kids want to go sledding?" Dad asked.

Mila frowned.

"But we don't have a sleigh!"

"You're so right! I guess we'll have to buy one," Dad said, and Mila's face lit up. Then he clipped his leash to my collar.

"Let's go, Charlie," Dad said.

"Where are we going?" Mila started putting on her shoes.

Dad looked away.

"Charlie will stay somewhere safe and warm, where he'll be well cared for until we come back to get him."

"What do you mean, come back to get him?" Mila's voice shrilled. "He's not coming with us?"

"Not right now. But we'll come back and get him."

"When?"

Dad sighed.

"Soon."

Mom leaned to scratch my ears.

"I'm sorry, Charlie. I wish we could take you, but we can't. But I promise we'll come back for you," she said, and that was the last time I saw her.

Dad drove me to a new place, a long concrete house that smelled bitter, like fear. There, he handed my leash to a man in a green uniform and gave him the box with my stuff — my bed, my toys, even the smoked bone I had gotten for Christmas. I had chewed it only a little.

"These are Charlie's belongings," Dad said. "He's a good boy."

The man nodded and tugged on my leash. I looked at Dad.

"Dad?"

He turned around and walked away.

"Dad! Dad!" I barked, but he didn't look back. He kept going as if he couldn't hear me and reeked something awful.

A rancid smell of guilt and misery, as if he'd puked on the dining room carpet.

"Dad! Don't leave me here! Please!"

I jerked to follow, but the leash held me back.

"I'm so sorry! Dad! I only ate Tom's cookie by mistake! I thought it was mine. I won't do it again, I promise!"

Dad didn't answer. He didn't even glance back.

"Dad! Please!"

The heavy door slammed shut behind him.

5

―――――――

BEHIND BARS

I struggle to get to the door to follow Dad, but the leash stops me in my tracks. I pull with everything I have, desperate to get back to the car, but the man in green pulls even harder. I plant my paws on the concrete to dig in, but he drags me to another door and opens it.

The concrete room beyond isn't made for dogs like me.

The smell hits me like a ton of bricks before I even glance inside. The air is sharp with bleach, but it reeks of wet dogs, poop, and piss. Still, heavier than any is the stench of despair, so strong it takes my breath away. I'm not the only one who hates being here. Everyone does, even the human.

I freeze into place and dig my claws in, but the floor doesn't give. The human keeps pulling, and I skid on. The rough concrete scrapes my paws, so I move my legs to follow, though I want to run away. My ears droop with dejection, and my tail tucks between my legs until it almost touches my chin.

That's when the chaos begins. The initial terrifying silence shatters into a cacophony of howls, whines, barks, and growls coming from every cage in this hangar, and they are too many to count.

The long row of cells stretches into a blur. I look beyond the grates at the hundreds of eyes glued to me. Some are hostile, some curious. Some defiant, others defeated. A hundred noses stick out through the bars to sniff me and learn everything there is to know about me. Before I'm ten feet into the room, they all know that I'm six, a boy, healthy, and neutered.

But what they really want to know is if I'm someone they should respect and maybe even fear.

But I'm not. I'm just a pup. I'm too small to fight, too scared to growl, and too shy to bark back. I drop to my belly, drowning in shame. I hope the human lets me die here.

"Come on, Charlie," he mutters. He pulls me forward and drags me on the floor like I'm dead.

But I'm not. I just wish I were.

A white pit bull with a long scar along his right muzzle and half an ear missing lunges at the bars as I pass by. His eyes are blood-red; his bark is a gunshot.

"What are you doing here, boy?" he growls.

I'm too terrified to answer, so I melt into the floor, hoping he forgets about me, but he doesn't. He keeps growling, cursing, and barking, even when I'm a dozen cages away.

"Don't mind Killer. He's more bark than bite," the human says, but I'm so terrified I piss myself, and the entire shelter smells it. Every one of these dogs witnessed my shame, and I can't even run and hide.

The man keeps dragging me as a scruffy fox-terrier glares at me down his nose and growls something I don't catch. A big, one-eyed mutt barks as I pass. I want to puke. I can't take this anymore, so I glue my eyes to the floor to avoid anyone's gaze.

"Fresh meat, huh?" An evil-looking brown mutt jumps on his door, rattling his cage. I crouch to the floor, terrified he will get me, but he doesn't.

"Don't you worry, pipsqueak. You'll get used to it," he barks.

I'm not worried. I'm way, way worse. My mouth is so dry I can't bark. And what would I tell them, anyway?

The man finally stops at an empty cage. He opens the screechy door, throws in my bed and my bone, then shoves me inside.

There's some straw on the floor, and a water bowl in a corner. I crouch to lap some water to relieve my parched throat. The man unclips my leash. He slams the door shut with a bang, then walks away before I even get to ask what's going on.

Oh, no!

"Please, mister, please!" I yap. "This must be a mistake! I don't belong here, you see. I have a family! I belong with Mom and Dad. And Mila and Tom! Please! Can you..."

The hangar door closes behind him.

He's gone.

He left me alone with my misery and a million barking dogs.

"Who are you, boy? Look at that silly orange mutt! I'd be darned if he doesn't smell of shampoo! He's even got a bone! Aren't we special? I bet he's not coming from the streets!" a deep bark comes from my left.

"And he's got a bed! A proper bed, not just straw! Just look at that," someone yaps.

"That wouldn't last long if I got my teeth into it!" someone growls to my right.

"Neither would he," a nasty voice answers. "Just sniff him and you'll know he's a coward."

I curl up in my cage with my back against the concrete wall and close my eyes. I refuse to look at them, and I act like I can't hear them, though of course I do. I can smell them too. Their stench of bitter fear and bullying and rage flips my stomach. I wish I could hold my breath.

There isn't a nice one in the bunch, I think, when a touch of kindness hits my nose. I lift my eyes to see a strange fellow straight across from my cell. He's tall and big-chested, with a long, narrow muzzle, and a wide head. His brindle coat looks like it used to be white, but it got washed with the colored clothes and dyed unevenly. His half-folded ears look like an afterthought, but his amber eyes look at me with kindness.

"How ya doing, kid?" His voice is gruff but gentle. His long, heavy tail rattles his cage when he greets me with a wag.

"I've been better," I whimper.

"Sure you have. We all have. But this is not as bad as it looks. They're just excited to see someone new because not much happens here. Other than when someone comes or goes. Those pooches make a lot of noise, but they'll simmer down in no time and get back to napping and cleaning their privates. Just ignore them."

"But I can't!"

"You'd better learn, or your life will be awful. In times such as these, the best thing to do is to live inside your head. What's your best memory?"

"My best memory?"

"Yeah. A day you were so happy you couldn't believe it. Where were you and what were you doing?"

"I was at the beach with my family. The kids flew a kite, and I chased them. We swam, and then Dad and I played fetch. And we ate cold chicken and donuts."

"There now. Close your eyes and stay there. Smell the salty wind, listen to the waves and taste that chicken; hear the kids' laughter and feel the sand under your paws. Stay there until you're ready for this."

"But I will never be ready for this. I don't want to be here."

"Of course not. None of us do, but we are, aren't we?"

His calm voice gives me courage.

"Thank you for your kindness, sir. Who are you? And what are you, if you don't mind my asking? You look... different."

"My name's Lambo, from Lamborghini. I'm a greyhound."

I wag my tail in thanks.

"Sir, would you mind telling me what happens next?"

He sighs and lays his nose on his paws.

"Well, first you'll sit here and wonder how your life got so bad. Then, if you're lucky, a human will come by. If he likes your face, he'll take you home. If you're not... oh well."

He doesn't finish, but his eyes glaze over and his ears flatten. The rancid stench of despair coming from his cage tells me that whatever comes next, I don't really want to know. And I don't.

I don't even want to think about how my life got so bad that I ended up here.

All I want is to go home.

6
____

SHELTER

Lambo was right. Before long, the other inmates forgot about me. They went back to their business, which consisted of teasing each other about this or that, taking long naps, and cleaning their private parts.

"I told you they aren't bad folks," Lambo said, licking his hind paw, which he did often. "They're just showing off to the newcomers. And to each other. But when you get to know them better, they're not unfriendly. Sniffing the breeze together helps time go by; otherwise, days stretch forever. Even Killer, who's the worst of the lot, isn't that bad. It's not his fault he was bred to fight."

I cock my head left to hear better.

"What do you mean, he was bred to fight?"

"Killer is a pit bull. That wasn't his choice, just like it wasn't my choice to be a greyhound, and it wasn't your choice to be a... What are you, by the way?"

"Mom said I'm a poodle mix, but I don't know which."

Lambo studies me carefully.

"You're curly, and the right color, but you're too small to be a Goldendoodle or a Labradoodle. A cockapoo, maybe? Are you hypoallergenic?"

I cock my head the other way.

"What's that?"

"I don't know, but it seems to help with adoptions. Lots of people look for hypoallergenic breeds, whatever those are. How old are you?"

"Six? Or seven? I'm older than Mila, and she's four."

"You're not that old, but you're no longer a puppy. Everyone wants puppies, so they go like hotcakes. Nobody wants older dogs."

He smells bitter again, so I do my best to distract him.

"You were telling me about Killer?"

"Yep. So, he was bred to fight, and he was brought up to be angry and mean."

"But why?"

"Because his human had him fight other dogs, and he wanted him to win."

I cock my head back from right to left to hear better, but I still don't understand. Mom always praised me when I got along with everyone else at the dog park. The one time I growled at an uppity terrier who took my ball, she scolded me and took me home.

"But why? Why would his human want Killer to fight?"

"Because he bet on him. Whenever Killer won, his human made money."

"What's money?"

"Those stinky pieces of paper humans carry around in their pockets until they give them to someone else."

"What for?"

Lambo scratches his left ear with his paw, then shakes his head. His folded ears flutter.

"I'm not sure. But they seem to relish having them. When I was racing..."

"Racing?"

"Yes. My friends and I, we used to run around a race track chasing a lure. Whenever I was first, Buzz, my trainer, filled his pockets with money. That made him very happy."

"What's a lure?"

"It's something that attracts you to chase it. For us, it was a dusty mechanical rabbit. It smelled of mineral oil and screeched as it ran by."

"What did you do with it when you caught it?"

Lambo smells his paw, then licks it clean.

"I never caught it, really. Nor did anyone else."

"So why did you run after it, if nobody could ever catch it?"

Lambo sighs.

"Good question. I guess we just love to run? You know, Charlie, we greyhounds are bred to run, just like Killer was bred to fight, and like poodles... What were poodles bred for? What was your job before you came here?"

"I cleaned the dinner plates before loading the dishwasher. I also looked after the children. And cuddled with Mom and Dad whenever they smelled upset. That always made them smell better."

"Hmm. I don't know of any dogs bred for that. Maybe you were like a companion?"

I wag my tail.

"You got it. Mother said I was her best companion whenever she didn't feel well. I put my head in her lap and let her pet me, and that always made her feel better. The kids too."

"That's got to be it, then. Maybe you're just a companion breed, not a working one."

The long, low dog in the cage next to Lambo shakes his head.

"Absolutely not. Poodles were bred as hunting dogs. Their job was retrieving geese and ducks from the water for hunters. They pretend to be French, but they started in Germany. Even their name comes from the German word 'Pudel,' which means 'to splash in water.'"

"Wow! How do you know all this?" I ask.

The low dog looks at me down his long nose with an air of Teutonic superiority.

"Because I'm German and smart. That's how I know it."

"Modest too," Lambo growls, but he wags his tail to make it clear he's joking. "Charlie, meet Beethoven. Beethoven, meet Charlie."

I wag my tail politely, wondering what sort of dog he is. He's dark-brown, long and really low, with bright eyes like coffee beans and long shaggy ears that almost sweep the floor. How the heck does he even walk, I wonder, and check out his legs. They seem too short to let him scratch himself properly. Can you reach your ears with your paws? I'd like to ask, but I'm afraid that would be rude.

"Delighted to meet you," I say. "If you don't mind my asking, what breed of dog are you?"

"I'm a long-haired Dachshund." He holds his head up proudly. "My folks and I, we specialize in digging."

"Digging what?"

"Anything. Whatever you need dug, just call us and we'll

do it for you. We were bred as hunting dogs to chase and flush out badgers. That's where our name comes from. Dachs means badger in German; Hund, obviously, means dog. Everyone knows that." He gives me a severe glance.

"Obviously," I mumble, though I do not speak a word of German. Still, Beethoven seems mollified.

"That's why we have short legs and long, muscular bodies: to dig tunnels and crawl into them. But, more than anything, we were bred to be brave and tenacious. We're among the few creatures brave and strong enough to confront a badger. Did you know that even hyenas fear badgers?"

"I didn't. But I've met no hyenas. Not personally."

"Good for you. Those ugly creatures are better lost than found. They're stinky, ruthless feliforms who feed on dead bodies and don't hesitate to confront even lions. Still, badgers give them a run for their money."

I didn't even know that hyenas had money, I think, but keep that to myself.

"What's a feliform?" I ask instead.

"It's a cat-like animal. But they look and act more like dogs."

"Why?"

Beethoven gets a sudden urge to clean his tail. He curls into a pretzel and licks it thoroughly. When he's finally done, he looks at me.

"You were saying?"

I know this trick. The old "must clean tail right now" gives you time to gather your thoughts and find a good lie. But I don't want to embarrass him.

"You have every reason to be proud of your ancestry," I say, and I'd be damned if that grumpy Beethoven doesn't wag his clean tail. Fractionally.

When night comes, everyone goes quiet. There's no sound but a snore here, or a squeak there, where someone must be dreaming of a chase. I wish I could sleep too, but I can't. I'm too worried about my family.

Where are they? How are they? Who looks after the kids and cleans their dishes now that I'm not there? Who sleeps with Mila and licks her nose in the morning when it's time to wake up?

They may come to get me tomorrow.

The thought gives me hope.

They sure will; they can't leave me here, can they?

That night, I chased the kids in my sleep.

7

REVELATION

They didn't come.

They didn't come the next day either. Nor the day after that.

I wake up full of hope every morning. Whenever the door opens, I listen for their steps. Whenever someone comes, I sniff to catch their scent.

It's not them.

Every night, I tell myself they'll come tomorrow. They must be busy moving. It takes the kids forever to put away their toys, so they need a few days to get settled. They'll come to get me tomorrow.

I know they will.

How could they not? They are my whole life, and they love me just as I love them. Leaving them behind would be like losing my tail. That can't happen. They're on their way; I know it. They'll be here any moment.

While I wait, I chat with my new friends.

"How did you end up here?" I ask Lambo.

He sighs, and a dank smell of sadness wraps around him like a cloud. Humans don't know it, but we dogs can always smell how they feel. The scent of emotions comes out of them like the smell of cooking drifting out of Mom's kitchen. Every feeling smells different, just like foods, condiments, and spices.

Sadness is moldy and damp, like an old basement; fear is rancid, jealousy sour, and anger sharp and hot, like firecrackers. Other feelings smell good: Joy smells like a sun-warmed meadow where you can't resist chasing your tail; hope smells like a crisp summer morning as you get ready for a walk; and love smells best of all, like a muddy puddle after rain that you can't wait to jump into.

"He got hurt and can't race anymore," Beethoven growls, "so his human dumped him."

"It wasn't like that." Lambo shakes, but his bark lacks conviction. "He tried. I hurt my paw during a race, and Buzz took me to the hospital. I had surgery, then rehab, then..."

"Then what?" I ask.

"Then... he didn't come back to get me."

"Of course not," Beethoven growls. "He didn't need a pet. He needed a greyhound that could win races, so he probably got another dog."

"No, it's not like that. It's complicated." Lambo looks away, and I can smell he doesn't want to talk about it.

"It's not complicated at all," Beethoven barks. "That's how humans are. They keep you as long as you're useful, or at least cute, then they dump you. That's pretty much what happened to every dog in this place. Other than the street dogs who never had a home, they all got dumped. Now they all wait for someone to rescue them, but there are way more dogs in need than there are rescuers."

Lambo sighs.

"That's true. I've been here for months, and nobody looks at me twice. They all want puppies, or at least small dogs that are cute. Like you. And young. I'm too big, too old, and too ugly. Nobody wants me." Lambo yawns. He's upset. The smell of his despair chokes me.

"There'll surely be someone," I bark. "And you're not ugly. You're just... different," I growl, taking in his strange shape. His long, narrow muzzle doesn't match his wide chest and shoulders. As for those ears...

I change the subject.

"But this isn't too bad, is it? It's warm, and they give us food, and we get to sniff the breeze together."

"No, for as long as it lasts. But it doesn't last forever."

"Why not?"

"Because they must make room for the new ones."

"New ones?"

"Yes. The new dogs without homes. You know what a kill shelter is?"

"No."

"This is it. They keep you here and feed you and look after you, hoping that someone takes you home. But if nobody does, sooner or later they have to make room for the new ones."

"How? They put us two in a cage?"

That sounded so silly that even Lambo laughed, despite his sadness.

"No, Charlie. They put the old ones to sleep. For good. As in, those who cannot catch someone's eye and find a new family get killed."

It takes me a while to understand. When I finally do, the thought is so horrible it crushes me. That's impossible! Humans can't do that! Not after they look after you and feed you and even play with you!

"That can't be true!" I bark.

"Oh, but it is," Beethoven growls. "You just arrived, so you still have time, but Lambo and I are running out of chances."

I'm still trying to wrap my mind around the fact that a human could kill a dog they looked after, when the man in green comes in and the whole place goes quiet.

He brings no new dog, no water, and no food, so every dog in the hangar holds his breath, wondering what he'll do. The air is thick with the rancid fear of a hundred dogs, and every tail in the place is tucked in, but nobody looks the man in the eye. It's like if they don't look at him, he won't look at them either. They remind me of my kids.

The door screeches when he opens the door to Killer's cell. He clips his leash to Killer's collar, slips a muzzle on his nose, and scratches him behind his ears.

"It's time, old boy," he whispers. "I'm sorry."

"No! No! It can't be," Killer yaps. "I'll be a good boy. I won't threaten anyone today and..."

"Sorry, old boy. But it won't hurt."

"But..."

"So sorry, my friend."

"But please, please."

Killer pleads, squeaks and whines like a puppy, begging for mercy, but the green man doesn't relent.

The door slams behind them like a gunshot.

Chaos erupts. Every dog in the kennel barks, jumps, and

yaps all over each other in a frenzy. At first, I think they're upset, but the smell of their exuberance hits my nose, leaving me puzzled. They are thrilled. I know Killer wasn't the nicest dog in the shelter. Far from it, in fact. Still, it's sad.

"Why is everyone so happy?" I ask. "Did they all hate Killer so much?"

Lambo shakes his head so fast his silly ears float around it.

"No. They're just happy it wasn't them."

"Not this time," Beethoven growls. "But there's always next time."

"The next one is me," Lambo says, laying his nose on his paws.

"Why do you say that?" I ask.

"He's been here a long time," Beethoven says. "And I'm next."

He curls in a corner of his cage with his nose under his tail, smelling stale, like resignation. I find it hard to believe it.

"And you'll just take it lying down like that?"

"What else do you want us to do?"

"Fight it, for Dog's sake!"

"We're not fighters," Lambo says. "None of us are, but Killer was. See how much good it did him?"

Their calm surrender drives me mad. I get so angry that I can't sit still, so I start pacing through my cell, back and forth, back and forth, until my paws start hurting. That calms me down.

I sit down to think, but that's not working, so I decide to clean my private parts. That always helps me focus. This time too.

The idea pops into my head just as the green man brings our dinner. I watch him intently and sniff to see if he smells like Killer's blood. He doesn't. He only smells of sweat and kibble.

I wait until he turns around and leaves before growling at the boys.

"I figured out what we must do."

"What's that?" Lambo asks, but there's no hint of hope in his scent.

"We need to escape."

8

———————

ESCAPE

Beethoven stares down his long nose at me and wags his tail left in the dog equivalent of a sneer.

"Really? What a genius! I wonder why nobody else ever thought of that."

"Leave Charlie be," Lambo growls. "He means well."

"I know he does. It's just that he thinks we've all been sitting on death row cleaning our tails for Dog knows how long, and nobody came up with that brilliant idea. Only him."

My excitement melts like an ice-cream cone in the sun. I tuck my tail and hang my head, but Beethoven isn't done. He and his Teutonic disdain need to crush me completely.

"And how exactly do you propose to do it?" he asks.

"I... I didn't think about that."

"Think then. And let us know if you get any ideas."

They go back to sleep, but I keep thinking. I clean my private parts until they shine, then move to the tail, but I get no more ideas. So, I go to sleep too, hoping something will come to me tomorrow. Or the day after that.

But nothing does, and after a while, I start getting used to life in the shelter. I don't love it — how could I, without my family? But as day after day goes by and my family doesn't return, their memory starts fading. Every night, I think of their scents: Mom always smells of some sort of cooking and that silly spruce spray. Dad reeks of sweat, gasoline, and beer; the kids smell of peanut butter and chocolate. And shampoo, since they outgrew the baby powder.

But after a while, even their scents start fading from my mind. As I lose them a little more each day, it feels like my whole life before this shelter has been nothing but a dream.

The day the green man comes empty-handed again, we all freeze, desperate to see whose turn it is.

He turns towards us and Lambo's heartbeat goes crazy. So does Beethoven's. Mine too, but he stops at a big, one-eyed mutt named Kevin. Poor Kevin whines and screams and howls, but he gets dragged away. Watching that breaks my heart, but I still sigh with relief that it's not one of my friends. Or me.

But we know our time is coming.

I keep thinking of a way to escape, but nothing comes to mind. Other than our short daily exercise, we are locked in our cells day and night. And even when they take us out, we're never together. The fence around the yard is too tall for me to scale, even if it weren't topped with barbed wire. The only escape I can find is in my dreams.

Until tonight.

It starts with the silence.

Our windows are always half-open. For ventilation, they say. They're too high for us to see through them, but the wind and the scents still get in. That's how I know it's still winter.

But things feel different tonight as something strange seeps in. It's not a thing, not a noise, and not quite a scent. It's more like a ghostly touch that none of us can see, but we all lift our noses to sniff it.

"That's odd," Beethoven growls.

"What is?" I ask.

"The scent. It feels like a tornado."

I sniff and sniff, but other than car fumes and dust, I get nothing.

"Did you feel your ears pop?" Lambo yawns.

"I did."

"That's the pressure drop. Big storm coming."

"How do you know that?"

"You must have lived a sheltered life. You used to sleep inside, didn't you?"

"Of course. We only went out for walks."

Lambo laughs.

"No wonder you know nothing about the weather, then. A tornado is coming. A big one."

"What's a tornado?"

"It's a strong wind that twists and turns and blows away everything that stands in its way. Even cars, houses, and trees. It's a bad time to be outside."

"Good thing we're inside, then," I say, but Lambo and Beethoven shake their heads.

That's when I start feeling it too. The storm's power wraps around me like an itch, making me shiver. I need to run and hide, but I can't. I am locked in my cage, and getting away is not an option for me or the others. I shiver as my nose fills with the scent of the storm. It's dust and mud and the ozone's sharpness, but, more than anything, it's the rancid stench of fear coming from every dog in here.

Like that wasn't bad enough, horrible noises come in. The wind roars like a freight train at full speed, howling, whistling, and screeching. I'm so scared I can barely breathe.

That's when the door opens and the man in green rushes in.

He's empty-handed, but for once he's not alone. Another man in green opens the doors to our cages while the first one takes us out two at a time. Barred doors screech and bang shut; heavy boots pummel the floor; a hundred dogs yelp, whine, and bark, compounding the chaos.

"Where are they taking us?" I ask.

"They're evacuating us, but I think they're too late. They should have started hours ago if they wanted to keep us safe," Beethoven growls, watching the man open the cell next to mine.

"Now! It's time," he barks.

"Time for what?"

"Time to run, you dummy. Remember, you wanted to escape? Well, you'll never get a better chance," he yells as the man in green unlocks my door and moves on.

I freeze in place and watch him unbolt Lambo's door, then Beethoven's. The other man comes at us with leashes.

"Now! Go," Beethoven barks, and Lambo takes off like the supercar he's named after, so fast his tail is just a blur. I follow him with all I have.

The green man leans over to catch him. Lambo swerves without slowing down, and the man stumbles. He falls on his butt, cursing up a storm, then struggles to get up as I pass him at top speed. Beethoven's next, but his tiny short legs hold him back. He does his best, but by the time he gets there, the man has recovered enough to grab him by the tail.

"I've got you," he mumbles, and tries to slip a loop leash around Beethoven's friend's neck.

Without even thinking, I U-turn. I growl and snap my fangs one inch from his nose. He jerks back and drops the leash. Beethoven flies out, and I follow.

Thanks to the chaos, the doors are all open, so we follow Lambo's scent through the hallways and the mudroom, then dart through the entrance door into the driveway.

Oops! This is where Father parked the truck when he brought me. What if he's still here? I stop to check.

"Keep going! Don't stop now," Beethoven wheezes, his short little legs moving as fast as they can.

I sniff left and right to make sure Dad's truck isn't here. Nope. No trace of his scent, or the truck's, so I dart after Beethoven and Lambo. Before long, we leave the shelter out of sight, so we slow down to catch our breath.

This is the first time we're together without cages keeping us apart, so we proceed to sniff each other's butts in proper introduction.

That's when I get the shock of my life.

"You're a girl," I yap at Beethoven in wonder.

9

BEETHOVEN

"Thanks for letting me know, Mr. Oblivious," she barks, just as something crashes right next to my tail.

I jump away. An enormous tree crushed the house behind us and shattered it to pieces. Half the corrugated roof flies away, tumbling through the air like a plastic bag in the wind. The other half got flattened under the weight of that monster, whose trunk alone is bigger than our dining room table.

The wind howls and rages all around us, pulling at shingles like a mad dog shaking a bone. A white car tumbles by. A motorcycle follows. Pieces of broken wood, twisted metal sheets, and all kinds of stuff fly in all directions, carried by the wind, which can't decide which way to blow. The one thing it clearly wants to do is pull off my coat and steal my ears as I struggle to hold on to my tail. Beethoven is close to the ground, so she's safer, but Lambo would have flown away if he hadn't hit a brick wall. He shakes his head to get it together and tries to catch his breath as Beethoven barks orders.

"Let's shelter before we take off," she growls, and starts digging under that enormous fallen tree.

"What are you doing?" I ask.

"Getting us to a shelter. There."

Sure enough, before you could finish saying 'grass-fed beef kibble with wild rice,' she's dug a tunnel under the tree that leads to some basement stairs.

The passage is big enough for her and almost big enough for me, though I have to struggle hard to squeeze in, but it's way too narrow for Lambo. His shoulders get stuck, so we both start digging from inside to widen the tunnel enough to let him through.

And just like that, we're inside. The wind still howls out there, and terrifying noises come from every which way, but in here we're sheltered. Between the concrete staircase and the massive tree that's going nowhere, we're comfy and safe, so we lean into each other to share body heat. Poor Lambo needs it the most, since he's got like no fat and almost no coat worth mentioning. Soon enough, we're so cozy we lay our noses on our paws to share stories.

Beethoven fascinates me. Before I got to sniff her butt close and personal, I thought she was a boy, and I'm shocked. It's true that unless you're a bloodhound or at least a basset, you can't get someone's every detail without getting close to them, but I have never been so wrong. Mis-gendering someone? I hope the other dogs don't find out, or they'll laugh me out of the kennel.

"Would you mind telling me why you look like a boy when you're a girl on the inside?" I ask, wagging my tail politely. I'm worried she'll get into a funk. Of course, she does. Whether boy or girl, Beethoven surely can be grumpy.

"Boy, girl, what difference does that make, especially since you're neutered? All you should care about is what I can do. Can I choose the right moment, take the initiative, and dig tunnels? I can. Does my sex matter for any of that?"

"It does not."

"So, why do you want to know?"

Good question. Why do I want to know? How's that any of my business?

It's not.

So then?

I can't put my paw on it, but I think that's how I make sense of the world. Things are one thing, or they are not. Somebody is either a boy or a girl. They are either a dog or a cat. I am hungry, or I am not. Scratch that one, since I'm always hungry for the good things, though not for kibble.

But putting things in boxes is how I keep track of the world around me, even if it makes no real difference, like Beethoven said. It shouldn't matter if she was a squirrel. She's kept us all safe, and she proved herself worthy during our escape. That should be enough. Still, that silly itch inside me wants to know which box to put her in.

"I don't know why," I growl. "But you're right. It's none of my business. I am sorry."

"You should be." Beethoven glares at me down her long nose, which is also muddy from the digging. "But since you helped me escape when the guard grabbed me by the tail, I'll tell you. Still, next time you have the urge to stick your muzzle in someone else's affairs, remember it's none of your business."

"I will. Thank you."

"I was born a boy. Or so they thought. I was the pick of my

litter, so the breeder decided to sell me for breeding. He kept me until he found the right buyer, then I went to the new breeder. Still, my mom always had doubts. She knew better than humans. Dogs always do."

Lambo and I wag our tails. We've both met enough humans to understand how little they know.

"'Be yourself, dear. You're perfect just the way you are,' she said. 'But it turns out she was mistaken.'"

Beethoven yawns because of her sadness. Speedy and I yawn too, showing our empathy.

"I grew up in my new kennel. They fed me and treated me well, but when the time came to perform my duties, they found I wasn't interested. Not even a little bit. They put me with the best-looking female Dachshunds, but none of them stirred my heart."

Lambo and I glance at each other. The notion of a good-looking Dachshund, male or female, is hard to grasp, but we're smart enough to keep that to ourselves.

"We were friends, of course, and I bossed them around, but nothing happened. Surely not what the breeder expected. He took me to the vet, and I got a full exam, including genetic testing. Long story short, it turns out I have ambiguous genitalia."

"Oh," I say, as if I understand.

Lambo doesn't.

"You have what?"

"I have a condition called DSD. I'm a girl inside, but I look and behave like a boy. I feel like one too, to be honest. But the one thing I can't do is breed, so the breeder had no use for me. He could have sold me as a pet, but that would have made him lose money. So he surrendered me to the shelter instead to collect his insurance. That's how I got there."

"I'm so sorry," I growl.

"Me too." Lambo wags his tail.

"But I'm selfishly glad you were there last night. I don't know what we would have done without you."

"Me too," Lambo agrees. "Thank you for enlarging that hole so I could get in."

Beethoven measures him with her coffee-bean eyes and wags her tail a tiny bit.

"It is not a hole. It's a tunnel. But you're welcome."

10

GOODBYE

We stayed in that den until the world got back to its senses. It felt like forever, but when the wind stopped howling and hurling roof tiles, bicycles, and garbage cans, we decided it was time to get out.

We crawled back out to utter devastation. Nothing stands, as far as we can see. No house, no tree, no power lines. It looks like the place got ransacked by a mob of angry burglars. Debris of all kinds litters the ground. There's even a boat, though we're nowhere near the ocean; otherwise we could smell it.

"What a debacle! At least there are no dead bodies," Lambo growls.

"Not within sniffing range. They must have evacuated earlier." Beethoven shakes the dried mud from her coat and sniffs the wind.

"What do we do now?" Lambo asks. "Should we go back to the shelter?"

Beethoven glares at him.

"Are you nuts? If you thought you were on death row before, this makes it ten times worse. If the shelter looks anything like what's here, there's nothing to go back to. And even if it still stands, what do you think all the humans who used to live in these flattened homes will do with their dogs? They have no place to live, let alone somewhere to keep their dogs, so they'll surrender them to the shelter in droves. And you know the rule: first in, first out. That means bye-bye, Lambo and Beethoven. You, Charlie, might have a chance since you had just arrived, but we two are goners."

The thought of my friends being dragged out to be slaughtered like Killer and Kevin sends a chill through my body. I shudder.

"So then, if we don't go back to the shelter, what do we do?" Lambo asks.

"We head south. And we make extra sure the humans don't catch us to take us back. With a bit of luck, we'll find another shelter further south. There, we may get a reprieve, since we'll be the newcomers."

"But..."

"What?"

"What will we eat? And where will we sleep?"

Beethoven glares at him down her long nose and shakes her head.

"We'll sleep wherever we can, and we'll eat whatever we find. How about chasing some real rabbits for once, Champ Lambo?"

Lambo's ears flatten.

"I've never done that, you know. I have heard that my ancestors used to do it, but that was out of fashion before I got into the business. I'm not sure I can even run without a racetrack."

"Well, you'll have to learn, or you'll go hungry. Let's go," Beethoven barks.

"But..." I whine.

"What?"

"I can't go south. I have to go north."

Lambo cocks his head left, trying to understand.

"What for?"

"That's where my family went. Mom and Dad and Mila and Tom went north. That's where I need to go if I want to find them."

Lambo shakes as if he just took a mud bath.

"That's a lousy idea, kid. It's winter. Up north, it will be even colder. You may even find snow."

"That sounds like fun! I love snow," I bark.

"Not when you're living outside, you won't," Beethoven growls. "For once, this fast doofus got it right. Heading north now is a terrible idea. Why don't you go south with us, then you can turn around and go north as soon as the winter is over? There's power in numbers. The three of us together will fare better than if you went alone. We'll help each other through whatever comes our way; we'll defend each other and share body heat and food. Alone, you'll freeze to death, and you'll go hungry."

"It's either one or the other. It can't be both," Lambo mumbles, and Beethoven sends him a wilting glare.

"Yes, it can. Just not at the same time," she growls.

"Sorry, guys. I can't do it. I need to find my family. What if they need me? Who's cleaning the dishes and playing with the kids? Who looks after Mom when she's not feeling well?

Who greets Dad when he comes back from work? I need to go."

Lambo wags his tail left.

"Oh well. You need to do what you need to do," he growls, but I know he's not happy.

Beethoven shakes her head until her long ears slap her face.

"Listen, kid, that's an awful idea, and no human is worth it. I've never seen a human going hungry and risking freezing to death just to help a dog. Humans use you and abandon you, every single darn time. Look at Lambo here. As soon as his human stopped making money out of him, he dropped him like a hot potato. Same with my breeder. He didn't even bother to sell me, because he could make more money by putting me on death row. Your humans too. If they loved you and needed you, they wouldn't have thrown you away like a loaded poop bag. Don't be silly!"

My head tells me she's right, but I can't hear any of it. My heart has no room for anything but my love for my family. I can't listen to this wiener dog speak ill of Mom and Dad and the kids. That makes me so mad I want to rip her apart, but I manage to stay civil.

"Sorry, guys. No can do. Good luck with everything!"

I wag my tail at them one last time, though it's mostly left, and take off without looking back.

I head north.

11

CHARLIE'S JOURNEY

I run north without looking back, so mad I can't think straight. How dare this wiener speak ill of my family? She doesn't even know them! She hasn't seen Mom take care of me when I was sick, and Dad smell heartbroken when the vet had to wash my stomach. She doesn't know how the kids' faces light up when they see me, or how they always slip me food under the table. She knows nothing about them, but she feels entitled to blame them.

Lambo too! He didn't say much, but he stood right there and listened instead of telling her to mind her own business. It's like he agreed with what she said.

The more I think about it, the angrier I get, and that gives me energy. I'm so furious I keep running without even sniffing right and left to figure out where I'm going. All I want is to put more distance between me and my former friends. How dare they!

I run and run until my paws hurt, and my lungs feel ready to explode. When my anger chills a little, I stop to catch my breath and look around. I don't know where I am, but it's nowhere I've ever been or want to be.

Whatever this place used to be, it no longer is. The tornado ripped it apart like I ripped Dad's boot when I was teething. When I was done, you couldn't even tell whether it was the right or the left. Same here. Everything normal is gone. There's nothing but debris as far as I can see, most of it so broken I can't tell what it is. The ordinary scents are gone, too. No scent of cut grass, wood smoke, or mouthwatering barbecue. Not even gasoline fumes. This place stinks of charred plastic, spilled fuel, and waste. Stuff is strewn everywhere, but there's no living creature in sight. There's no one else here but me and my misery. And the silence.

By the time the shadows lengthen and the sun's strength fades, telling me that the night is coming, my anger has fizzled to worry. Where am I? My stomach growls, reminding me I haven't eaten in forever. I wouldn't mind some meatloaf even if there's no bacon, but I catch no hint of food. Not even kibble.

It gets colder and colder, and for the first time ever, I feel grateful for my curly coat. I used to hate it when Mom brushed me, but right now I wouldn't mind a second one. I'd even take those silly red pajamas with a hole for the tail they had me wear at Christmas, but nobody offers.

I don't know how far I ran, but it must be miles and miles. My soft paw pads that are used to polished floors, soft carpets, and freshly mowed grass, are so raw they're bleeding. At least they distract me from my empty stomach, I tell myself as I push on. Still, nothing can distract me from the emptiness in my heart. And what makes it worse is that it's my doing.

It's not my fault Mom and Dad left me behind — at least I

don't think so. I always tried to be a good boy. But I abandoned my friends. And that's on me.

I got so mad this morning that I ran away in a huff and left them behind, forgetting all they'd done for me. But for Lambo's kindness, I'd still be curled in that cage, hiding my nose under my tail, sick with fear. And if not for Beethoven, I'd be in that darn shelter, waiting to die. But I got so mad that none of that mattered. When I didn't like what they said, I took off without looking back. Instead of appreciating their care and well-intentioned advice, I just ditched them. That was dumb.

The shadows turn to darkness, and the cold becomes unbearable. The wind cuts through my coat like I'm bald and seeps into my bones. My hips ache. I slow down to a trot. Then a walk. Then a shuffle.

I need shelter for the night if I want to keep going tomorrow.

I smell water and follow my nose to a broken pipe. The puddle smells of gasoline, and the water tastes of rust. It's sharp on my tongue, but it's better than nothing. I drink until I feel full, then I curl up with my nose under my tail behind a crumbling wall. It's not warm, but it hides me from the worst of the wind.

Where is my family? How many more days like this will I have to get through before I find them? How many more days like this can I take? I'm cold, hungry, and lonely, and my heart aches with the need for a friend.

Where are Lambo and Beethoven? Did they get caught and dragged back to the kill shelter, or did they find a place to hide? Are they hungry and shivering, like me?

At least they're together. They have each other to lean into and share body heat and companionship. I have no one. Nobody to care about me, help me, or at least spare me a tail wag. I'm all alone, and the solitude crushes me.

I tell myself that tomorrow will be better. I'll get up early and go further. Who knows? Maybe before the sun goes down, I'll find Mom and Dad and the kids, and we'll be together again. How far could they go? I ran all day, so I must be at least halfway.

It will be better tomorrow, I tell myself, and fall asleep.

12

NEEDLES

It turns out I was wrong. I didn't find my family the next day. Nor the day after, nor the day after that.

I kept following my nose north, but each day got harder than the last. Beethoven was right. The further I went, the colder it got. Running kept me warm during the day, but at night? I crawled under porches, hid inside tool sheds, or squeezed under prickly bushes that tore at my skin. Still, the cold kept me awake. And in the little sleep I got, I dreamed about my family opening their arms to me, but I always woke up alone. Like now.

The ground is frozen. I shiver so hard that my teeth chatter, and try to stand, but my paws can't remember how it's done. It takes them forever to wake up and get moving.

I'm stiff and everything hurts. My paws sting from yesterday's blisters. My tongue tastes bitter from licking dirt, tree bark, and grass to cheat my hunger, but at least my empty stomach stopped growling. It got tired of asking.

I start north again.

It's harsher up here. The empty fields gave way to rocky hills. Patches of thick forest hide gurgling icy streams that try to steal you. There's still no food, but the water is good.

Yesterday I saw snow. I didn't know what the white stuff was at first. It fell from the sky as if someone shook a down pillow. I thought they were feathers, but when I sniffed them, they stuck to my nose and melted. They tasted of nothing, and they didn't fill my belly. They only froze my tongue.

The trees up here are still standing; I smelled mice and even squirrels, but I didn't see any. Didn't hear them either, though the woods are so quiet you can hear your heartbeat. There's only the whisper of the wind through the trees, and the crunch of the frozen snow under my paws. I keep my nose down to follow the animals' paths and tuck my tail between my legs to keep it warm, but there's nothing warm here. When was the last time I was warm, I wonder, when I catch a sudden whiff.

Of what? It's not food.

The scent of something wild is almost buried under the smell of rotten wood and dead leaves. Someone alive hides behind a rocky hump. But who?

It's not a bristling, threatening scent. It's the placid, steady smell of someone who belongs here. Whoever it is, this frozen forest is their home. What an odd place to live!

I follow my nose without stopping to think and find him behind a fallen log. Half-buried in leaves, a strange creature shaped like a toilet brush shuffles along, slow and deliberate. He doesn't care that his hair is a mess and doesn't run when he hears me. He doesn't even growl, just turns his head and looks at me.

I cock my head to see him better, then wag my tail in a friendly greeting.

"Hi. I'm Charlie," I bark. "Who are you?"

He doesn't answer. He doesn't wag his tail, but he doesn't growl either, so I get one step closer.

"I'm a poodle mix and I'm six. I ran away from the shelter, and I'm frozen. And hungry. Would you know of any food nearby?"

He just keeps staring at me with those beady eyes. Is he deaf?

"What kind of animal are you?"

Nothing.

Oh well. I may as well find out for myself. I step closer to sniff its butt in introduction.

BAM!

A sharp, blinding pain explodes in my nose, then another, and another. I yelp and jump back, then take off. When I'm far enough, I stop to shake my head, but the pain doesn't stop. It grows and spreads from my muzzle into my mouth and my tongue like liquid fire.

I paw at my nose. Something's stuck there, something that won't come off. It pulls and hurts and burns, and the pain makes me sneeze. A spray of blood reddens the snow.

What the heck was that? I glance back.

The thing doesn't chase me. It just turns its back on me and shuffles away.

Whining with frustration, I paw at my nose even harder, but that doesn't do me any good. My heart races, and blood roars in my ears as I panic. I shake again, but the movement only makes it worse. Something is stuck in my nose where I can't even bite it.

I stagger into the brush and curl up in the snow. I claw at my nose and thrash until I can't do it anymore.

When I open my eyes, the world is blurry. I sniff, and I regret it as soon as the fire shoots through my face.

I stick my tongue out to lick my nose and feel what's stuck in it. It's a needle, buried deep. I can't reach it with my teeth, so I rub my nose against the dirt to get it off.

Oh, how I wish Mom were here! Whenever I got burrs stuck in my paws, she took them out gently. I tried to pull away, but she held me still and got them all out.

But Mom isn't here. Nobody is.

I curl into a ball and cry until the cold creeps into my bones, my tears freeze stiff in my fur, and the pain settles into a dull thud.

I keep pawing at my face until one needle comes out with a sickening tug, then another. I yelp with pain, but keep going as blood drips onto the snow, melting it into dirty patches. I lick it off. What else can I do?

Lambo would have kept his distance. Beethoven would have sniffed it from afar and walked away. Not me. I ran into this fiasco, nose first, like I always do. I figured that if I want something, that means it's safe. I'm a loser.

The thought hurts almost as bad as those needles.

I drag myself under a thicket and press my nose into the snow to cool the burn. My muzzle hurts, my tummy is empty, and my heart feels hollow. I'm so exhausted I fall asleep.

I dream of my friends and of Mom's gentle hands petting me, but I wake to the cold, bitter truth. I'm alone, frozen, and so stiff I can barely open my mouth. But I still can walk.

So, I walk.

North. Always north. My family is there. I know it. And

Mom will take care of me when I get there. The sooner, the better.

I break into a run.

13

LIFE ON THE STREETS

I keep going. Always north.

Before long, the woods turn to pastures, and the roads become streets. I'm overjoyed to find houses and humans. Even dogs! My heart and my tail thump like crazy as I rush to greet them and ask if they've seen my family, but they don't want to be my friends. They only want what little I have: my shelter, my food scraps, my dignity.

I backed away and let them have them at first. What else could I do? But I soon learned that if I wanted to survive, I had to fight.

I didn't win. Not often. But day after day, I got leaner, meaner, and more desperate. I learned to choose my battles. Fighting a yappy Chihuahua over a half-eaten cookie left me with a bloody ear, an empty stomach, and terrible shame for running off with the tail between my legs. The street mutts chasing me made me wary of talking to strangers, especially when they're in a pack. Oh, how I miss Lambo and

Beethoven! They're not the world's greatest fighters either, but being together beats being alone.

I met humans. Not mine, but humans still. Some threw me a bite of their sandwich or the crust of their pizza; some threw stones. Sometimes you get lucky; sometimes you don't. An old woman fed me a bowl of warm stew on her porch. It smelled of onions and beef and love, just like Mom's cooking. That was the best food I had since I left home. When I saw a man loading boxes smelling of fresh pastry into a truck, I wagged my tail and got closer. I hoped he'd spare one for me, but he cursed and kicked me as if I had wronged him. I limped away, but the rock he threw at me left a dent in my muzzle.

For every friendly face, two are mean. For every good day, three are bad. But I learned to tell the kind humans from the others. I don't know if it's in their eyes, their voice, or their scent, but I rarely get fooled anymore. The dogs, however, have all been mean. I haven't met a friendly pup since I left Lambo and Beethoven.

The other day, a long truck almost ran me over, then blared its horn as its draft threw me into the gutter. I picked myself up and shook, worse for the wear, but that taught me to look both ways before crossing the street.

That served me well. Last night I hid by a river under an old wooden bridge. I nestled in a pile of dirty rags and fell asleep.

I'm dreaming of my family when a feral smell wakes me up. My heart starts racing before I'm fully awake, and I wonder where that musky scent comes from when I see two gray shapes slink my way.

Coyotes.

They creep closer and closer, muzzles sniffing the air, fangs gleaming in the moonlight. Two pairs of scary yellow eyes glow in the darkness.

I crouch and freeze in place. My ears flatten and my tail tucks tight. Should I run? A small pup like me doesn't stand a chance against these monsters. I can't fight them.

My heart thumps so hard I fear they'll hear it.

They get closer, following my scent like I follow the aroma of bacon. One sees me and growls, harsh and low. The other wags his tail, happy to find dinner.

They found me. I have to take my chances.

I jump up and dig my claws into the slippery mud to scramble up the wet bank. Growling and grunting, they lunge after me. I see a gap where a board is missing from the bridge. The beast on my heels snaps his fangs just an inch from my tail, but with the strength of desperation, I dig my claws into the rotting wood and squeeze through.

The gray muzzle with ugly sharp fangs follows me, but he's too big to fit through, so they take the long way over the bridge. I run as fast as I can, but I still glance both ways before darting across the highway.

Tires screech. Horns blare. Someone screams and wails right behind me, but I'm already on the other side. I leap headfirst into the ditch.

I pant and listen, shaking like a leaf.

Nothing.

When I finally crawl out of that ditch, the sky has started to fade. I'm frozen and bleeding, but alive, and a strange thought crosses my mind.

I'm struggling, of course I am. But I'm learning.

I shake and keep going north. Always north.

14

THE CAT

It's snowing. The sun has set for another long night as I cross an empty road and my stomach growls, reminding me I've had no dinner. No lunch or breakfast either. I'd better find something, or I'll be too weak to walk tomorrow.

I raise my muzzle to sniff for info. I catch a whiff of smoke to my left. Smoke means humans, and that's where food lives. I might find something if I'm careful. It's not exactly in the right direction, but I'll make a course correction later.

I run as fast as my tired paws will take me. Before long, I see houses, but they have fenced yards and barking dogs telling me to get lost. I do. There's rarely food in people's yards, and never when there's a dog.

I keep going until I sense a dumpster. A good one too, by the aroma of burgers and fries. There's got to be a fast-food place nearby, but it's late, and it's probably closed. I'll just see what I find in that dumpster, I tell myself, and sneak to it on my toes. You never know with dumpsters. The local dogs see them as theirs, and it's not wise to encroach.

I sniff, but I smell no dog and no human, so I dig right in. I rummage through plastic bags and garbage until I find a cardboard Big Mac package. That's something I wouldn't say no to when I'm hungry and it's soggy with fat, but for now, I'll hold off for something better.

And there it is: a whole cheeseburger. A bite is missing, and it's disassembled, of course, but who cares about aesthetics? The cheese stuck to the meat, and so did most of the ketchup. Wow! I slobber so hard it hurts and open my mouth to swallow it whole — I'm not a big one for manners — when I catch a whiff of something funky.

Eat first, investigate later, I tell myself, ready to wolf down the burger, when something hisses above me. A piercing wail shreds my ears, and a set of sharp claws grab my collar before digging into my shoulder to the bone.

I yelp and jump back, but the thing won't let go. Needle-like teeth sink into my ear and a claw rakes my face, aiming at my eye. I leap away, but the thing sticks to me like a steel trap, wailing like an ambulance with lights and sirens. I try to shake it, but it hangs on, hooking onto my shoulder.

My heart races. I get dizzy with fear. What is this? I have never been so terrified, not even during that awful tornado. This, whatever it is, wants to eat me alive. It takes another bite of my ear. Crazy with fear, I throw myself to the ground and roll in the snow.

The thing hisses, sneezes, and lets go. I jump to my paws and take off before it can grab me again, ignoring the burger aroma. I dash across the street and hide behind the bushes before looking back. What the heck was this?

I can't believe my nose. Nor my eyes.

It's a cat. I'd be darned if it's not a cat. Not a big one either, just half my size and striped, with a scarred face, sharp ears, and half its tail missing. This is un-freaking-believable! I got beaten, robbed, and utterly humiliated by a cat!

I've never met a cat before, not personally, but I've seen them on Mom's Facebook. Aren't they supposed to be cute and cuddly? How on earth did I stumble upon this devil?

She finishes my burger in no hurry, then licks her chops. She sits on her butt and cleans her paws like she doesn't have a care in the world, licking every claw from the root to those sharp, bloody tips she dug into my back. When she's done, she proceeds to clean her ears with her front paws, again and again. I'd be darned if she doesn't look my way as if she knows I'm hidden behind that bush.

"Keep away from me, you silly mutt, if you want to stay alive," she seems to say, then turns around and leaves with dainty steps, as if she hates touching the snow.

I wait until she's out of sight before returning to the dumpster to eat the Big Mac box. I chew every bite and lick the place where it sat, but I'm still hungry when I'm done. But there's nothing left, so I squeeze under the bushes and shiver through the night as the snow piles on top of me.

The morning finds me frozen, hungry, and hopeless. I thought I was learning to survive, but I was wrong. I'm just a useless coward. How can I hope to find my family when I can't even hold my own against a cat? And why would they want a coward like me?

I'll walk into town and find the local shelter. I don't deserve any better, I tell myself, limping with the burn in my shoulder.

15

A HOME

I'm hungry, hurting, and frozen to the bone as I drag myself along the town's main street sniffing for the dog shelter. I've never been there, but I know how it smells: like terrified dogs and despair. It shouldn't be hard to find.

It's early morning. Nobody pays attention to me. Angry snowplows roar down the road, spitting dirty snow to the side. Trucks and cars plod up and down, sliding on the icy patches; harried humans, bundled to their eyes, shovel driveways and steps piled high with snow.

I limp on, sniffing left and right for that cursed shelter, but that's the one thing I can't find. Everything else is here: the bakery, whose warm, buttery aroma gets my belly growling with hunger; the coffee shop, smelling bitter of coffee; the gas station, reeking of gasoline and fumes; the hairdresser, by the scent of hairspray. Everything's here but the shelter.

Now what?

This is awful. I'm so useless I can't even find the dog shelter. More hopeless than ever, I sit in the snow looking up and down the road, wondering what to do next, when a door opens across the street.

"Hey, pup. Come here," a woman says. I look to see who she's talking to, but there's nobody here but me.

"Come here, boy." She slaps her thigh. Maybe, just maybe, she's talking to me? I wag my tail tentatively, ready to take off as soon as she picks up a rock. But she doesn't.

"Come on, now, or we'll freeze the whole house."

I glance right and left and cross the street. Still wary, I sniff her way, but she doesn't smell like hate. She smells of cooking. That reminds me of Mom, and my heart melts.

She scratches my ear, the one that the cat hasn't chewed on, and lets me inside. I panic when she closes the door, but she opens the fridge and the scents coming out make me dizzy: bacon, cheese, and bologna.

A few heartbeats later, she sets a bowl of steamy mac and cheese in front of me. The buttery, cheesy aroma makes me slobber so hard my tongue hurts, but I sit and look up for permission. She laughs.

"Go ahead, baby. I knew you weren't a street dog even before I saw your collar," she says. "You must be lost. Let's find your people, okay?" She checks my tag while I devour the food.

I inhale it and lick the bowl clean, then look up for more. She shakes her head.

"I'd give you more, but I'm afraid you'll get sick. Wait a bit, okay?"

I wag my tail and start sniffing around. Grape jelly! Peanut butter! Johnson shampoo! That can only mean one thing: children! There are children here! This is almost as good as home! I wag my tail a mile a minute as two girls in pajamas gallop down the stairs. They're about as big as Mila, and they both Ooh! and Aah! when they see me. Before long, we're playing fetch with their socks like old friends.

I can hardly believe my luck. Only this morning I was looking for the shelter; now I'm warm, with food in my belly, and I have kids to play with!

The woman gets off her phone and gives me another bowl of food. I'm finally full, and happier than I've been since home.

The girls and I are chasing each other around the dinner table when the doorbell rings. The woman opens, and two men in green step in. I don't know them, but I know their smell.

My stomach flips.

"I called the number on his collar, but it's disconnected. I didn't know what else to do, so I called you."

"Thank you for doing that, Ma'am. Nice pup. It would be a shame if he got hit by a car or froze to death in the streets," one man says, while the other slips a loop around my neck and tightens it. I try to run, then turn to fight, but the other one slips another loop. Two heartbeats later, I'm stuck between two leashes like a convict.

The girls cry. Their eyes teary, they plead with their mom.

"Can we keep him, Mom? Please? Pretty please?"

She shakes her head.

"We can't. I'd love to keep him, but our lease doesn't allow pets."

"But, Mom..."

"I'm sorry, sweetheart. We can't have a dog here. If we kept him, we'd have no place to live. But he'll be all right. These gentlemen will take him to the shelter, where they'll look after him and find him a new home. He's such a nice pup; he'll have no trouble getting adopted."

Oh, yeah? Tell that to Lambo and Beethoven, I think, as the men drag me out.

The little girls are still crying at the door as I get loaded into a crate and the van takes off. Before you can say: "Who's a good boy?" I'm at the shelter.

16

NEW SHELTER

It's not the same shelter. Neither are the dogs, but they smell just the same. Their stench of fear, rage, and despair takes my breath away as I get dragged to a cell. A foaming Rottweiler jumps on his door to rattle his cage and bark curses at me. A mean-looking black mutt growls a long string of insults, besmirching my lineage. A pit bull covered in old scars threatens to rip me apart and eat my beating heart. I stagger under the cacophony of smells and angry threats as I follow my captor to an empty cage. Everything is just like the last time.

Everything but me. I'm no longer the same dog.

Last time, I got dragged on the floor in my walk of shame between cages. I was terrified to the bone of the angry dogs that barked and lunged at me. I was so scared I pissed myself.

But I've learned the ropes. Now I know that every one of these dogs, no matter their color, size, or breed, is just as scared as I am. They all fear they'll be the next to go when the place runs out of room.

Like that's not bad enough, they allow cats here. Sickening! Why would they bring those filthy demons here? Aren't we miserable enough?

I discovered that the more I learn about dogs, the less I fear them. Not so with cats. My respect for those creatures verges on terror. I wouldn't go near them if you offered me an entire meatloaf wrapped in bacon. I dread them even from afar. I know their evil magic spills beyond their cage, and they sense my terror and thrive on it.

The headman here is a woman named Ella. Ella reminds me of Beethoven, though she's not a Dachshund and doesn't have long ears. Not even a tail. But she growls just the same, and something about her self-assured grumpiness feels familiar.

When the men in green brought me in, Ella cleaned my wounds gently but firmly, then brushed me. I tried to run. After living on the streets for Dog knows how long, what's left of my coat is a tangled mess, and brushing it hurts.

"You. Sit. Still," she barked.

I did. I put up with the ordeal, whining only a little. Then she petted me and gave me a treat.

"You are a good boy, Charlie. Good-looking too, especially if those bald patches grow back. I bet we'll find you a new home in no time."

I believed her because I wanted to. I started hoping again.

But nothing happened. New dogs came and went. Some got adopted, but more and more of those who'd been here before me crossed the rainbow bridge to make room. Before long, I was no longer the new dog in the shelter. I was the old one that nobody wanted. My hopes grew thinner and thinner each day.

I was sleeping with my nose under my tail when the men in green brought in a new inmate and put him in the cell across from mine. We got acquainted, even though we couldn't smell each other's butts to introduce ourselves properly.

He's a handsome fellow named Ranger. He must be some kind of Golden Retriever, so he's orange too, which made me like him on the spot. That may not be a good reason, but it's no worse than us both being inmates, with nowhere to go and nothing to do but clean our privates and chat. So chat we did.

We have more in common than our color. Ranger also comes from the streets, and he fought his share of losing battles. But we're not the same.

Ranger is not afraid of cats. Well, he didn't say he was, which is pretty much the same thing. More importantly, he doesn't want to get adopted. He doesn't want a home, and that astounds me. He doesn't even know what a home is.

I tried to explain, but I must have done a lousy job, because he still wants no home and no family. All Ranger wants is his freedom.

"What is freedom?" I ask.

He gets so excited that he jumps to his feet and starts pacing. He can't pace far because our cages are just three feet wide, but he goes through the motions.

"Freedom is when you can go where you want, when you want. You let your nose be your guide and follow your heart to whatever adventure awaits you. You sleep when you're tired and wake up when you're ready. And you can raid every dumpster in town."

I wag my tail left.

"I didn't think dumpster diving was that much fun."

Ranger looks down his nose at me.

"It's an acquired taste. The technique takes some getting used to, but once you master it, it's awesome fun."

I have my doubts, but who am I to disagree? I'm not the dumpster master. He is.

"So, what else about freedom feels so good?" I ask.

He sighs.

"When I stretch my legs and run, my chest fills with air, my legs pump the ground, and my paws eat up the pavement. I feel like the master of the world. It's like the earth belongs to me. I can jump in any puddle and stay there, or roll in the snow if I want."

I am befuddled. It turns out that all that time I tracked north, frozen and hungry, looking for my family, I was in fact living in freedom. I could go anywhere I wanted, whenever I wanted, and nobody told me what to do. I could roll in the snow all day if I wanted, but why on earth would I want to? The one time I did it was to get rid of the cat, and that was one time too many. I shudder. To each his own.

I yawn discreetly to express my disagreement, but he notices, of course, and piles up more.

"I can chase squirrels and bark at cars and sleep until noon if I want."

"Sure you can, but don't you get lonely? Who plays with you? Who loves you? Who do you love?"

Ranger stares at me as if I've grown a third ear.

"I play whenever I want. Thing is, I love my freedom more than I could ever love a human. They're ruthless, heartless, and useless creatures that kill for fun, like cats. I've never had any good coming from a human."

My heart aches. That's pretty much what Beethoven said,

and I left her and Lambo in a funk. But by now I've learned better than to break up with a friend over a difference of opinion. Especially when they're right.

I loved my humans with all my heart. I did my best to be a good boy and to look after them. All I wanted to do was make them happy. And where did that get me?

17

ESCAPE

Ranger taught me much about dogs and humans. About life, even. Sniffing the breeze with him made the days fly like the wind. I selfishly hoped he'd stick around until I found a home. Or crossed the rainbow bridge. I didn't want to be alone again.

But life tricked us, as it always does.

Ranger wanted nothing but his freedom, while I still hoped against all hope to find a home. That's why, the day that old wheezy human came to visit, I put myself out there. I wagged my tail in doggy smiles; I jumped on the door, and I tried my best to look cute. Right across from me, Ranger snored with his nose under his tail. He didn't even bother to open his eyes.

No matter how much I wanted, I didn't get adopted. I would have traded my tail for a loving human to look after, but no.

Ranger did.

"I came to take him," the man said.

Ella crossed her arms over her chest. Her crisp laundry scent turned to the bitter smell of burned toast, so I knew she disapproved.

"I don't know about that. Ranger can get frisky, you know. That dog is too smart for his own good. And he hates cats."

The man laughed, then broke into a cough so heavy I worried he'll choke.

"Who doesn't? I hate cats too."

Ella shrugged, unconvinced.

"Why don't you have a look at Charlie here? He's such a good boy! Smart and handsome, too. He'll make a great pet. He'd keep you company and need very little work. He..."

The man shook his head.

"No, thanks. I want my boy, Ranger. I owe it to him. You know I shot him by mistake? I went hunting, and I thought he was a bear. When I saw I'd almost killed him, I ran him to the vet. I couldn't sleep for days until he got better. He looks just like my old boy. Ranger's the one I want."

Ella sighed.

"If you're sure..."

"I'm sure."

Before you could say "pig's ear," the man clipped a leash onto Ranger's collar and took him away. The door slammed behind them, and my buddy was gone. Just like that. I didn't even get to say goodbye.

My heart ached so bad I couldn't stop yawning. Once again, I had missed my chance to get adopted. Ranger did, though that was the last thing he wanted. How awful for us both! What will happen to me? And how will Ranger feel in his new home? Will he learn to love it, or will he miss his freedom?

I'll never find out, I told myself. I curled up in a corner to sleep off my dejection when the commotion outside made me jump to my feet.

Ranger barked.

"Good luck, Charlie."

Someone screamed. Something thudded. Ella shouted, "Ranger! Ranger!"

A car door slammed shut.

Ella and the man come back without Ranger. They smelled sour, like spoilt milk and disappointment.

"I'm really sorry," the man said, then broke into a cough. "I should have listened to you. You were right; that Ranger is frisky. I couldn't imagine he'd try to escape. I was sure he'd jump in the car. It never even crossed my mind he'd turn around and run away like that. I wonder why."

Ella sighed.

"He's a handful, that one. I already called Animal Control. I hope they can catch him, but they've been on his tail for ages. Anyhow. If you still want a dog, why don't you look at Charlie here, as I said? He's such a good boy."

My ears perk up. Maybe? Did Ranger's escape buy me another chance?

The man shook his head.

"Sorry, I can't. I have my heart set on Ranger. I'm sure Charlie's a good boy and such, but he's not Ranger. Let me know if they bring him back, okay?"

Ella and I watched him leave with heavy hearts.

"Sorry, Charlie," she said. "I know you're disappointed. I am too. But there'll be someone else, you'll see."

I wagged my tail, but I no longer believed her, so it went mostly left. Still, I knew she meant well.

Th night comes. I can't sleep, but for once I don't think of myself or my family. I think of Ranger. Where is he? How is he? Is he happy he got the freedom he yearned for, or is he shivering under some bush, wishing he went home with that human who wanted him so?

I don't think so. If there's one thing I learned about Ranger, it's that nothing matters to him as much as freedom. Not the food, not the shelter, nor having someone to love. All Ranger wants is to feel the wind in his nose as he flies over the open spaces. And that's what he got.

For how long? Who knows? But for now, he's free. And happy. I hope.

I curl in a corner, waiting for the morning, but I keep an ear out for the van in case it brings Ranger back. My heart is torn, and my mind restless.

Did I get it all wrong?

What if Ranger is right and the only thing that matters in life is freedom? What if the only person you should trust is yourself?

I lived my whole life seeking the approval of my humans. I loved them, looked after them as best I could, and almost died trying to find them, even after they ditched me like spoiled leftovers.

Was my whole life a waste? And will I squander whatever time I have left waiting for some human to take pity on me? Or will I do something with myself?

But what?

18

HUMAN SHELTER

Awful days followed. I'd lost Ranger, the one friend who stood between me and loneliness. Even worse, I'd lost hope. I had nothing left to live for.

I was so lonely and dejected that I stopped eating. I got so skinny that my coat felt too big. Even worse, I started scratching and couldn't stop. Day and night, I chewed at myself and scratched myself bloody, as if the pain in my body could mask the deep ache in my soul.

Not only did I mourn losing Ranger, but my heart was torn with guilt for abandoning Beethoven and Lambo. I did that for the love of my family, who I now know lied to me and abandoned me on death row.

And whose fault was that? Every dog worth his kibble warned me not to place my hopes in humans. Did I listen? No. I ignored them. Even worse, I scorned them. And look at me now.

No more. I'm done with trusting humans and expecting

them to be loyal. It took me forever, but I finally understood that loyalty, truth, and selflessness are for the dogs.

Humans must come from cats.

But that doesn't make me feel any better. I'm just skin and bone and scabbed all over, but I can't resist chewing my nails until they bleed.

Ella worries.

"Stop that, Charlie! You were such a handsome little fellow, and look at you now! Stop scratching and start eating, or nobody will want you."

But I'm no longer listening to humans. Even Ella, who cares, lied to me. She promised to find me a home, but she didn't. So, I keep ruminating, starving and hurting myself. Every day I get worse, but I no longer care.

I sleep all day and dream about raiding dumpsters with Ranger, running over the wide-open fields with Lambo, or digging tunnels with Beethoven. They all have something to live for. But me? What do I live for?

Not a thing.

So, when Ella brings this woman to see me, I pay her no mind. I no longer care about humans. I just steal a quick sniff to confirm she's not Mom, then turn the other way.

Still, Ella will not be deterred.

"This is Charlie. He's in desperate need of a mission. He's just the pup you need."

The woman smells bitter, of coffee and doubt. She measures me with wary eyes and scratches her head. A strand of grey hair escapes from her messy ponytail, and she pushes it behind her ear.

"I don't know, Ella. He doesn't look well. Does he have

mange? I can't take a sick dog to those old folks and risk getting them ill, you know. That's the last thing they need."

"Charlie is not sick; he's just depressed, Marie. The vet checked him every which way. His best friend escaped and left him behind. He's lonely and bored. He needs something to do that will keep him interested."

Marie seems unconvinced.

"I really don't know. He looks like he can barely walk."

Ella shrugs.

"So what? How far does he need to walk to keep up with your seniors? I didn't think they ran around much."

"They don't, but..."

"Listen. Marie, why don't you give him a chance? Take him for a few hours and bring him back. This is not what we usually do, but I'll make an exception for you. And for Charlie. He's a great pup, and I know they'll love him. Just try him for a few days, okay?"

Marie sighs. I can smell she doesn't want to, but Ella will not take no for an answer.

"If you're sure..."

"I am. There." Ella clips a leash to my collar and hands it to her, then scratches me behind the ears.

"Be a good boy, Charlie. I have faith in you."

Faith? What's that? I wonder as the woman takes me to her car.

We stop at a big white building with a garden surrounded by a tall wrought-iron fence. It looks fine, but it stinks of dejection, and I wonder why.

I sniff around to figure out. The place smells of pine floor cleaner and cooked cabbage. And the fake air fresheners humans hang to mask odors - as if you can hide scents when you breathe them in all the time. But underneath it all, this place smells like the shelter: sour abandonment, bitter sorrow, and rancid despair. But I catch no whiff of dogs. What on earth?

Then it dawns on me: This is a shelter for humans.

We go inside. A few humans sit around a droning TV. They seem asleep. Nobody even looks at us.

This isn't like our shelter. There are no locked cages, just wheelchairs and sofas. And nobody barks at us. I don't think they even notice we're here until Marie claps her hands.

"Wake up, everyone! Look who came to see you! George, Wendy, Bob! Say hello to our guest."

19

———————

SENIORS

The humans open their eyes and turn towards us one by one. Slowly, very slowly, their vacant faces come to life.

The old man in the wheelchair speaks first.

"What is that?" The white hair floating around his head is so thin you can see his shiny pink scalp, but his big mustache makes up for it. He smells like stew cooking up in a bathroom.

"You tell me. What is this, Wayne?" Marie asks.

Wayne stares at me, trying to remember where we met.

"It's a dog." The small woman staring at me over her wire-rimmed glasses wears a black dress with a white lace collar. She reaches her hand towards me.

"Very good, Ruth. It's a dog. His name is Charlie."

I wag my tail and sniff Ruth. She smells of cookies.

"A dog?" The white-eyed woman in a wheelchair looks at the door behind me.

"Yes, it's a curly orange puppy. Would you like to touch him, Wendy?"

Wendy smiles.

"I would."

Marie walks me to Wendy's side. She takes her hand and places it on my back. Wendy gasps.

"He's so soft!"

Icy thin fingers run through my curls. She pets me gently while I sniff her and look into her eyes. They aren't quite white, but light blue, so light they look like ice. She still stares behind me, but her smile widens.

"May I touch him?"

Wayne's puzzled expression has turned to wonder.

"Certainly." Marie takes me to him, and Wayne pets my head with knotty, gentle hands.

"Ginger," he murmurs.

"Who?" Marie asks.

"A dog. I shot the geese, and she brought them out of the water. I called her Ginger."

The others stare at him in shock.

"I've never heard him string so many words together," Ruth says. "He makes sense, too."

"I'm glad you remember Ginger, Wayne." Marie touches his shoulder. "Good for you."

I disagree. It doesn't look good to me. He smells sad, like burned rubber. Fat tears run down his cheeks and soak his mustache.

"She died. Ginger died," he sobs.

I try to squeeze under the sofa, but he holds on to my collar. His tears stop as suddenly as they started.

"Charlie," he says.

I lick his hand to comfort him while struggling to make some sense of this.

Something is wrong with these humans. Whether they

smell like cookies, stew, or piss, they all stink of despair. And loneliness. They hate being in this shelter just like we hate being in ours. But what are they doing here? Who abandoned them? And why?

Are they waiting for someone to take them home, like we do? If nobody does, will their keepers send them across the rainbow bridge?

I have more questions than answers as I get to meet them one by one.

Ruth slips me half a cookie, and Marie pretends she doesn't notice. Then Bob, who walks with a walker, and Joe, who uses a cane, take me out for a potty break. They show me the garden. There's not much to see, since the snow isn't all gone, but just to be polite, I sniff the rocks and the bushes before doing my business. No hint of dogs, but I catch a whiff of a cat. My ears flatten and my tail tucks in, but fortunately, no cat shows up. Minutes later, we're back inside. Bob and Joe need to rest.

"We need to go now," Marie says.

Everyone protests, even Wayne.

"Why so fast?" Ruth asks.

"This is Charlie's first day on the job. We don't want to overwhelm him, do we? But we'll be back tomorrow."

Job? I didn't know this was work. It wasn't that bad.

On the way back, Marie gives me a long look.

"Well done, Charlie. You are a good boy."

I am a good boy? My ears perk up and my tail twitches. It's been forever since anyone told me that.

"How did it go? How did Charlie do?" Ella asks.

"Better than I expected. He was calm and polite, and

nothing fazed him. He tolerated their advances and behaved like a little gentleman."

A rare smile lights Ella's face. I'm so shocked I do a double take.

"I knew it. I knew Charlie was perfect for the job."

"Even more surprising was how they all came to life. Even Wayne, who hasn't spoken in weeks, remembered his old dog, Ginger. Bob and Joe, who won't get off the sofa for their therapy, took Charlie out. Even Wendy, who's been terribly depressed since she lost her vision, had a smile on her face. Your little Charlie was a miracle worker. They can't wait for him to return tomorrow."

Ella nods.

"Good. How about you, Charlie? What did you make of all this?"

What do I think of all this? It's complicated. Too complicated to explain.

But for the first time in ages, I feel needed. Those humans need me more than I need them. Having me there helped them remember the good times. I brought smiles to their faces and joy to their hearts, and I gave them something to look forward to. They can't wait for me to return tomorrow.

I wag my tail.

Neither can I.

20

SIX MONTHS LATER

It's a sunny fall morning as I wake up in Ruth's room. I sleep in a different room every night so everyone gets a chance to have company. I didn't love it at first, since I like my routine and I'd rather have my own spot, but what can you do? A job is a job, and it's not always fun.

But I make up for it by bringing my blanket, and they make up for it by sharing their snacks. Ruth has cookies, Bob has beef jerky, and Wendy has peanuts.

Ruth opens her eyes and smiles when she sees me.

"What a good boy," she says. "Wanna go potty, Charlie?"

"I really do," I bark. I've been crossing my legs to not bother her, but it's becoming rather urgent.

She opens the door. I wag my tail in thanks and sprint down the steps, then struggle to squeeze through the doggy door. I need more exercise. I'm watering the roses when Bob comes out. Since we walk every day, his hip got so much better that he ditched his walker for a cane.

"Charlie! How's it going?"

I wag my tail.

"Great, thanks. And you?"

"Never better. How about some breakfast, my friend? I'll share my bacon."

"That's a thought."

I follow him to the dining room, where half of the seniors are already seated. Joe sees us and frowns.

"It's not your day, Bob. Today is my day to have Charlie."

"Tonight, you mean. But during the day, he's free to spend time with whomever he chooses."

"I'll be with you in a moment," I tell Joe, chomping on Bob's bacon before going to greet everyone as I do every morning. I sniff them to see who needs me the most. Humans have good days and bad days, just like dogs. By their smell, I can always tell who needs a pick-me-up and give them extra time.

I spent a lot of time with Wayne before he crossed the rainbow bridge, but he left with a smile on his face. I worry that Wendy's turn is coming, so I do my best to soothe her and make her feel loved. But new folks come in all the time. Mildred's children brought her here when her husband died, and they never come to visit; Lorna got in an accident, and they took her car keys. Without her car, she can't live in her old house anymore, so she's here. When Betsy's leg turned rotten and the doctors cut it off, she came here too.

They're all despondent when they come. They lost their homes and their old lives, so they aren't even sure who they are. And they have nobody to tell their sorrow to.

After a while, they get used to being here and forget. They think of it as their home. And, in a way, it is.

But I remember. I remember being dropped off at the

shelter and waiting for my family to come back. Every morning, I hoped that was the day. Every night, I went to sleep hoping they'd be coming tomorrow.

They never did, and they won't. And I'll never forget.

People tell them: "You'll get used to it and you'll be fine," or: "We get cheesecake and a movie on Saturdays," or: "It's better than being alone."

But I don't. Because I remember.

I lean against their legs and put my head in their lap, even when I'd rather take a nap. I listen to their stories, lick their tears, and eat the treats they give me, even if I don't want them, because that helps them feel better.

Just like dogs, humans need to feel wanted and loved. Or at least useful.

I give them that.

I just give back what they gave me. This is not my home, and they are not my family, but they make me feel useful. Loved, even.

"Hey, Charlie?" Mildred glances at me over her dark-rimmed glasses.

I perk my ears.

"Yes?"

"How about some bacon?"

"On my way."

I've already had three strips, but it is what it is. If I puke, I'll clean up later.

～

To find out what happened with Lambo and Beethoven read **LAMBO** Book 4 in the **AMAZING DOG STORIES** series.

ABOUT THE AUTHOR

If anyone bothered to write it, Rada Jones's life would read like a thriller overindulging in twists and turns. Born in Communist Romania, ten miles from Dracula's purported castle, she trained as a mechanical engineer and designed gearshifts for tractors before working as an occupational therapist in a children's hospital.

She later met her American husband and immigrated to the US, where she embarked on her medical career.

For years, she worked shifts in the ER, then cruised the world's oceans as a ship doctor before eventually retiring to northern Thailand, the place of her dreams.

That's where she and her husband live their golden years, caring for a rolling assortment of stray cats and kittens they smuggle in and foster back to health before finding them forever homes.

Why cats and not dogs, you ask? Because her condo doesn't allow pets, and cats are easier to hide. They also bark less.

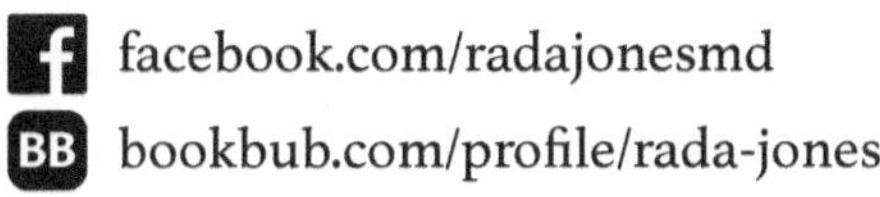

BOOKS BY RADA JONES

ER CRIMES Series — Gritty medical thrillers based in the ER and on cruise ships featuring Dr. Emma Steele, a sarcastic ER doc with a complicated family life and a great thirst for red wine, and a variety of serial killers, some nicer than others.

SOON TO BE X: An exotic adventure/romance describing a mature couple's unraveling after colliding with Thailand and their well-earned metamorphosis.

VELVET FILES — A gorgeously written series of breathtaking, gritty Thai-based crime thrillers. Not for the faint of heart.

K-9 HEROES Series — A team of opinionated bomb-sniffing K-9s tell their stories from the Afghan war and beyond. Like most war stories, they are not meant for young children.

AMAZING DOG STORIES — A series of novellas where ordinary pups tell their extraordinary tales. They'll make you laugh, cry and see the world in a new way.

STAY AWAY FROM MY ER: Heartfelt essays from a tired pit doc.

DRIVING ITALY: A cheeky travel memoir through Corsica, Sardinia, Sicily, and Italy. Featuring two senior curmudgeons driving a big car on Europe's narrow roads and showcasing mouthwatering food and wine, amazing art, and a bit of history.

EXPLORING KENYA: A cheeky safari memoir featuring ill-tempered rhinos, bickering lionesses, dominatrix hyenas, and playful hippos. Plus the intricacies of Maasai marriages.

THE SAGA OF THE DRACULA BROTHERS Series written as RR Jones: The gritty Mediaeval saga of the real Dracula brothers: Vlad

Tepes, Radu cel Frumos, and Mircea Dracula. The historically accurate story is richly textured and spiced with Transylvanian folklore but lacks vampires.